ASTERIX IN SPAIN

TEXT BY GOSCINNY
DRAWINGS BY UDERZO

TRANSLATED BY ANTHEA BELL AND DEREK HOCKRIDGE

HODDER DARGAUD
LONDON SYDNEY AUCKLAND

ASTERIX IN OTHER COUNTRIES

Australia	Hodder Dargaud, Rydalmere Business Park, 10/16 South Street, Rydalmere, N.S.W. 2116, Australia
Austria	Delta Verlag, Postfach 10 12 45, 7000 Stuttgart 1, Germany
Belgium	Dargaud Bénélux, 3 rue Kindermans, 1050 Brussels, Belgium
Brazil	Record Distribuidora, Rua Argentina 171, 20921 Rio de Janeiro, Brazil
Canada	(French) Dargaud Canada, Presse-Import, 307 Benjamin Hudon, St Laurent, Montreal, Quebec H4N 1J1, Canada
	(English) General Publishing Co. Ltd, 30 Lesmill Road, Don Mills, Ontario M38 2T6, Canada
Denmark	Serieforlaget A/S (Gutenberghus Group), Vognmagergade 11, 1148 Copenhagen K, Denmark
Finland	Sanoma Corporation, P.O. Box 107, 00381 Helsinki 38, Finland
France	Dargaud Editeur, 6 Rue Gager-Gabillot, 75015 Paris, France (titles up to and including Asterix in Belgium)
	Les Editions Albert René, 26 Avenue Victor Hugo, 75116 Paris, France (titles from Asterix and the Great Divide onwards)
Germany	Delta Verlag, Postfach 10 12 45, 7000 Stuttgart 1, Germany
Greece	Mamouth Comix Ltd, Ippokratous 57, 106080 Athens, Greece
Holland	Dargaud Bénélux, 3 rue Kindermans, 1050 Brussels, Belgium (Distribution) Betapress, Burg. Krollaan 14, 5126 PT, Jilze, Holland
Hong Kong	Hodder Dargaud, c/o Publishers Associates Ltd, 11th Floor, Taikoo Trading Estate, 28 Tong Cheong Street, Quarry Bay, Hong Kong
Hungary	Egmont Pannonia, Pannonhalmi ut. 14, 1118 Budapest, Hungary
Indonesia	Penerbit Sinar Harapan, J1. Dewi Sartika 136D, Jakarta Cawang, Indonesia
Italy	Mondadori, Via Belvedere, 37131 Verona, Italy
Latin America	Grijalbo-Dargaud S.A., Aragon 385, 08013 Barcelona, Spain
Luxemburg	Imprimerie St. Paul, rue Christophe Plantin 2, Luxemburg
New Zealand	Hodder Dargaud, P.O. Box 3858, Auckland 1, New Zealand
Norway	A/S Hjemmet (Gutenburghus Group), Kristian den 4des gt. 13, Oslo 1, Norway
Portugal	Meriberica-Liber, Avenida Duque d'Avila 69, R/C esq., 1000 Lisbon, Portugal
Roman Empire	(Latin) Delta Verlag, Postfach 10 12 45, 7000 Stuttgart 1, Germany
Southern Africa	Hodder Dargaud, c/o Struik Book Distributors (Pty) Ltd, Graph Avenue, Montague Gardens 7441, South Africa
Spain	Grijalbo-Dargaud S.A., Aragon 385, 08013 Barcelona, Spain
Sweden	Hemmets Journal (Gutenberghus Group), Fack, 200 22 Malmö, Sweden
Switzerland	Dargaud (Suisse) S.A., En Budron B, 1052 Le Mont sur Lausanne, Switzerland
Wales	(Welsh) Gwasg Y Dref Wen, 28 Church Road, Whitchurch, Cardiff, Wales
Yugoslavia	Nip Forum, Vojvode Misica 1-3, 2100 Novi Sad, Yugoslavia

Asterix in Spain

ISBN 0 340 14934 5 (cased)
ISBN 0 340 18326 8 (limp)

Copyright © Dargaud Editeur 1969, Goscinny-Uderzo
English language text copyright © Brockhampton Press Ltd 1971
(now Hodder and Stoughton Children's Books)

First published in Great Britain 1971 (cased)
This impression 92 93 94 95 96

First published in Great Britain 1974 (limp)
This impression 92 93 94 95 96

Published by Hodder Dargaud Ltd,
Mill Road, Dunton Green, Sevenoaks, Kent TN13 2YA

Printed in Belgium by Proost International Book Production

GAULISH VILLAGE

COMPENDIUM

LAUDANUM

AQUARIUM

TOTORUM

ARMORICA

BELGICA

LUTETIA

SPQR

GAUL
(ROMAN CONQUEST)
50 B.C.

CELTICA

PROVINCIA

AQUITANIA

e year is 50 BC. Gaul is entirely occupied by the Romans.
ell, not entirely… One small village of indomitable Gauls still
lds out against the invaders. And life is not easy for the
oman legionaries who garrison the fortified camps of
torum, Aquarium, Laudanum and Compendium…

a few of the Gauls

Asterix, the hero of these adventures. A shrewd, cunning little warrior; all perilous missions are immediately entrusted to him. Asterix gets his superhuman strength from the magic potion brewed by the druid Getafix...

Obelix, Asterix's inseparable friend. A menhir delivery-man by trade; addicted to wild boar. Obelix is always ready to drop everything and go off on a new adventure with Asterix – so long as there's wild boar to eat, and plenty of fighting.

Getafix, the venerable village druid. Gathers mistletoe and brews magic potions. His speciality is the potion which gives the drinker superhuman strength. But Getafix also has other recipes up his sleeve...

Cacofonix, the bard. Opinion is divided as to his musical gifts. Cacofonix thinks he's a genius. Everyone else thinks he's unspeakable. But so long as he doesn't speak, let alone sing, everybody likes him...

Finally, Vitalstatistix, the chief of the tribe. Majestic, brave and hot-tempered, the old warrior is respected by his men and feared by his enemies. Vitalstatistix himself has only one fear; he is afraid the sky may fall on his head tomorrow. But as he always says, 'Tomorrow never comes.'

TODAY, MARCH 17 TH, 45 BC (LATER, OF COURSE, ST. PATRIX DAY.), ALL IS PEACEFUL IN THE LITTLE GAULISH VILLAGE WE KNOW SO WELL. THIS TRANQUILLITY IS ABOUT TO BE DISTURBED, HOWEVER, BY EVENTS FAR AWAY IN LOWER HISPANIA ...

FRESH FISH – IT'S LUVERLY!

WHO'LL BUY MY FINE FISH?

HOW ABOUT SOME, FOR A CHANGE?

A CHANGE FROM WHAT? I'VE ONLY EATEN TWO BOARS SO FAR TODAY!

UNHYGIENIX FISHMONGER

ONE YEAR AFTER HIS VICTORY OVER THE SUPPORTERS OF POMPEY AT THAPSUS, CAESAR HAS JUST MOPPED UP THE SURVIVORS AT MUNDA*, BRINGING THE WHOLE OF HISPANIA UNDER THE ROMAN YOKE ...

LEGIONARIES, CAESAR IS PLEASED WITH YOU!

* MONTILLA

BEFORE GOING BACK TO ROME, WHERE A GREAT TRIUMPH AWAITS HIM, JULIUS CAESAR INSPECTS HIS OLD GUARD, THE GLORIOUS X TH LEGION.

THIS CHARMING GESTURE ASTONISHES SOME IBERIANS WHO HAPPEN TO BE WATCHING.

¡AY, HOMBRE! ¿WHY ARE THEY LENDING HIM THEIR EARS?

I THINK HE HAS THEIR EARS BECAUSE HE FOUGHT SO WELL

AND THE IBERIANS, BEING A PROUD AND NOBLE RACE, ARE ALWAYS READY TO ADMIRE BRAVE WARRIORS.

¡OLÉ!

WELL, WELL! MY OLD LAURELS, ALL CRUMPLED UP! I MUST HAVE RESTED ON THEM ONE NIGHT, BY MISTAKE!

AVE, CAESAR!

AVE, AVE, MY DEAR FELLOW! SO IT'S VENI, VIDI, VICI ONCE AGAIN, WHAT, BY JUPITER!

NOT QUITE VICI YET, I'M AFRAID, NOT QUITE VICI...

THERE'S A LITTLE VILLAGE, NOT FAR FROM MUNDA, WHOSE INHABITANTS ARE REFUSING TO INTEGRATE WITH THE ROMAN WORLD. THEY STILL HOLD OUT...

I KNOW, I KNOW... THEY STILL HOLD OUT AGAINST THE INVADERS. I'VE SEEN THAT SOMEWHERE BEFORE!

I SHALL LOOK INTO THE MATTER PERSONALLY. I MUST HAVE PEACE IN THE PROVINCES. TAKE ME TO THEIR LEADER!

SOON AFTERWARDS...

AND YET THE NATIVES SEEMED QUITE INDIFFERENT TO OUR SQUABBLES

THEY WERE PROBABLY WAITING TO SEE WHO WON SO THEY'D KNOW WHO TO HOLD OUT AGAINST

¡HALT, ROMANS!

WELL NOW, IT APPEARS THAT YOU WANT TO HOLD OUT AGAINST US?

¡THAT'S RIGHT! ¡AS LONG AS WE ARE HERE YOU WON'T HAVE A MOMENT'S PEACE!

¡OLÉ!

YOU'LL DO NOTHING OF THE SORT. WE'RE HOLDING YOUR SON AS A HOSTAGE. AS LONG AS YOU AND YOUR PEOPLE BEHAVE YOURSELVES, NOTHING WILL HAPPEN TO HIM. OTHERWISE...

OUCH!

¡IF I HAD YOU HERE, ROMAN, I'D HAVE YOU FRIED IN OLIVE OIL!

NOW, NOW! KEEP YOUR HAIR ON...

... OR YOU'LL SOON BE HEIRLESS. AS LONG AS YOU GIVE US NO TROUBLE, YOUR SON WILL BE QUITE SAFE

¡AY, WHAT BAD LUCK CHIEF!

¡YES, HOMBRE! MY ONLY CONSOLATION IS THAT THEY'LL HAVE THEIR WORK CUT OUT WITH THAT BOY

LATER...

WHAT SHALL WE DO WITH THE HOSTAGE, O CAESAR? IT WOULD BE DANGEROUS TO KEEP HIM HERE

QUITE SO. WE MUST SEND HIM AWAY FROM HISPANIA... THERE ARE A FEW GARRISONS IN GAUL WITH VERY LITTLE TO DO. DELIRIUM, FOR EXAMPLE

YOU MEAN TOTORUM, O CAESAR

THAT'S IT. HAVE HIM SENT THERE STRAIGHT AWAY, AND SEE THAT HE'S WELL LOOKED AFTER. IF ANYTHING HAPPENS TO HIM, THOSE RESPONSIBLE WILL ANSWER FOR IT WITH THEIR HEADS!

DOGMATIX AND I ARE OFF BOAR HUNTING! ARE YOU COMING, ASTERIX?

COMING, OBELIX!

THE ROMANS ARE KEEPING VERY QUIET!

OH WELL, THEY'VE BEEN BEATEN UP SO MANY TIMES THEY'RE FED UP

THAT'S RIGHT. WE'VE FINISHED OFF OUR OWN LOT... DO YOU THINK WE COULD WRITE TO JULIUS CAESAR AND ASK HIM TO SEND US SOME NEW ONES?

MEANWHILE, IN ANOTHER PART OF THE FOREST...

NO, NO, AND FOR THE THIRD TIME NO! YOU'VE RUINED THE WHOLE JOURNEY WITH YOUR WHIMS! YOU'VE BITTEN US, YOU'VE GOT US DOWN, YOU'VE WORN OUR NERVES TO SHREDS...

5A

AND NOW WE'RE ALMOST AT TOTORUM YOU WANT TO STOP AND PLAY! NO!

¡DON'T FORGET, O SPURIUS BRONTOSAURUS, IF ANYTHING HAPPENS TO ME YOU'LL ANSWER FOR IT WITH YOUR HEAD!

SO?

SO I'M GOING TO HOLD MY BREATH UNTIL SOMETHING DOES HAPPEN TO ME

HEY!

STOP! ALL RIGHT, WE'LL PLAY IT YOUR WAY!

PHEW! I BREATHE AGAIN!

5B

9

WE'LL TAKE YOU TO OUR VILLAGE

WHAT'S YOUR NAME?

¡HUEVOS Y BACON! I COME FROM HISPANIA

OOOUCH!

HE BIT ME!

I AM THE SON OF A CHIEF. PEOPLE OUGHT TO SHOW ME RESPECT. DADDY SAID SO

GRRRRR!

VERY WELL, SON OF A CHIEF, WE'LL TAKE YOU TO THE TOP MAN IN OUR VILLAGE!

GRGNNNNN.... RESPECT! HUH!

SOON AFTERWARDS...

AND WHY WERE THE ROMANS AFTER YOU, MY LITTLE ONE?

¡WHAT A BIG NOSE YOU HAVE!

GRGMFFFFF!

OBELIX!

HUMPH! TAKE HIM AWAY! WE'LL GO ON WITH THIS CONVERSATION AFTER MY AFTERNOON NAP!

MEANWHILE, IN THE TENT OF CENTURION RALICUS HALLELUJACHORUS, OFFICER IN COMMAND OF THE FORTIFIED CAMP OF TOTORUM...

HARD LUCK, BRONTOSAURUS! WHEN CAESAR HEARS THAT THE GAULS HAVE GOT HOLD OF YOUR HOSTAGE, YOU'LL BE FOR THE CIRCUS!

IS THAT SO? AND SUPPOSE I TELL CAESAR THAT YOU DIDN'T HELP ME TO RECAPTURE THE HOSTAGE, WE'D MAKE A FINE DOUBLE ACT IN THE CIRCUS THEN!

YOU'RE REVOLTING!

A GOOD THING TOO! IT'S MY ONLY CHANCE WITH THE LIONS!

THE BATTLE IS SHORT, OWING TO THE CLEVER MANOEUVRES CARRIED OUT BY THE LEGIONARIES, NOTABLY A SKILFUL WITHDRAWAL TOWARDS PREVIOUSLY PREPARED POSITIONS...

FOR A FEW OF THEM, HOWEVER, THERE WAS NOT ENOUGH TIME TO MANOEUVRE...

WHAT WAS THAT?

THAT WAS A WORD OUT OF PLACE!

MEANWHILE..,...

THE ROMANS REALLY WANT THIS CHILD! I WISH I KNEW WHY!

YOU'D LIKE TO KNOW THE REASON WHY WE'RE FIGHTING TOO, WOULD YOU, CHIEF?

WELL, SONNY? TELL US WHAT BROUGHT YOU FROM HISPANIA TO GAUL

MY DADDY IS THE STRONGEST DADDY IN THE WORLD AND SILLY OLD JULIUS CAESAR IS FRIGHTENED OF MY DADDY AND SILLY OLD JULIUS CAESAR HAD ME BROUGHT TO GAUL TO FRIGHTEN MY DADDY BUT THAT WON'T STOP MY DADDY BASHING SILLY OLD JULIUS CAESAR

¡OLÉ!

A HOSTAGE! HE'S A HOSTAGE! WE MUST PROTECT HIM FROM THE ROMANS. HE MUST NOT LEAVE THE VILLAGE!

OBELIX! I'M HANDING THIS LITTLE TERROR OVER TO YOU. AND DON'T FORGET THAT AS YOUR GUEST, HE'S SACRED!

YOU MEAN HE'S A HOLY TERROR?

WHAT'S YOUR FIRST NAME, SON OF A CHIEF?

PERICLES. WE'VE GOT SOME GREEK ANCESTORS. AT HOME THEY CALL ME PEPE

14

WHOSE IS THIS FISH THAT LANDED IN MY FACE?

?

IT'S HIS. HE HIRED IT OUT TO ME!

LOOK HERE...

PLAFF!

SLAP! SLAP! SLAP!

MISSED! YOU MISSED!

YOU MI...

THAT'LL TEACH YOU TO THROW FISH AT PEOPLE'S HEADS!

PLAFF!

?

BONK!

YOU KEEP OUT OF THIS!

POC!

HEY, BOYS, A FIGHT!

COME ON! IT'LL BE A CHANGE TO FIGHT EACH OTHER!

¡OLÉ!

WOOF!

PEPE MAY BE A NUISANCE, BUT HE'S BEEN HITTING IT OFF WELL WITH DOGMATIX SINCE THE FIGHT!

PEPE IS A BAD EXAMPLE TO DOGMATIX! HE'S YOUNG AND EASILY LED... SOMETIMES THEY WHISPER TOGETHER AND LOOK AT ME AND GIGGLE...

WE USED TO GET ON WELL TOGETHER, ME AND DOGMATIX, AND NOW...

WAIT A MINUTE! I THINK I'VE GOT IT...

O BARD CACOFONIX, WOULD YOU LIKE TO LOOK AFTER PEPE AT YOUR PLACE?

IF HE'D LIKE TO COME, IT WOULD BE A PLEASURE!

SOON AFTERWARDS...

I SHALL NOW SING YOU SOME LULLABIES TO SEND YOU TO SLEEP!

SURE ENOUGH....

I'M DREAMING OF A WHITE SOLSTICE...

?!

¡OLÉ! ¡IT REMINDS ME OF HOME, ESPECIALLY THE GOATS! ¡ANOTHER ONE, HOMBRE, ANOTHER ONE!

CLAC!

ROCKABYE, PEPE, ON THE TREE TOP...

YOU KNOW, ASTERIX, I'M BEGINNING TO THINK IT IS OUR MORAL DUTY TO RESTORE THAT CHILD TO ITS PARENTS

YES, IT'S A QUESTION OF MORALE

WONDERFUL, WONDERFUL DUROVERNUM... I CAN'T STAND IT ANY LONGER! BACTERIA! BRING ME A FISH...A BIG ONE!

THE ONE THE CHIEF HIT YOU WITH?

NEXT DAY...

WHERE IS YOUR VILLAGE, PEPE?

¡ I DON'T KNOW WHERE IT IS, BUT IT'S THE BEST VILLAGE IN THE WORLD AND MY HOUSE IS THE BEST HOUSE IN THE VILLAGE AND YOU STILL HAVE A BIG NOSE!

THOSE ARE NOT ADEQUATE DIRECTIONS...

IF HE'S TOO SMALL TO TELL US WHERE HE LIVES, IT'S GOING TO BE TRICKY TAKING HIM BACK HOME

THE ROMANS KNOW WHERE HE LIVES. WE ONLY HAVE TO ASK THEM

GOOD IDEA! THEY'VE STATIONED LOOK-OUTS ALL ROUND OUR VILLAGE, SO WE WON'T HAVE FAR TO GO

SOON AFTERWARDS...

WE MUST CHOOSE TREES WITH PLENTY OF FOLIAGE AND A GOOD VIEW OF THE VILLAGE. THEY'LL PROVIDE THE BEST PICKINGS

LET'S TRY THIS ONE!

AHA! THIS LOOKS LIKE THE PICK OF THE BUNCH!

TCHRAC

BOOM!

WHERE EXACTLY DOES THE HOSTAGE COME FROM?

HIS VILLAGE IS A LITTLE WAY TO THE SOUTH OF HISPALIS.* CAN I GET BACK UP MY TREE NOW?

* SEVILLE

HEY! ASTERIX!

THEY'RE NOT SO BIG HERE, BUT THERE ARE MORE OF THEM! SHALL WE TRY ANOTHER TREE?

NO, OBELIX. I'VE GOT ALL I NEED TO KNOW. COME ON!

PAF!

HEY!

POC!

BOOM!

IT DOESN'T TAKE MUCH TO GET YOU DOWN

I FEEL READY TO DROP....

OBVIOUSLY THE GAULS HAVE DECIDED TO TAKE THE HOSTAGE BACK HOME

AND SOMETHING WE SAID MUST HAVE TOLD THEM WHERE HE LIVES...

SO WE'D BETTER NOT MENTION IT TO OUR COMMANDING OFFICER...

THAT'S RIGHT! LET'S GET BACK UP OUR TREES!

18A

WE'RE NOT NUTS!

AND WHILE EVERYONE AT TOTORUM SEEMS HAPPY...

I SHALL SOON BE REJOINING MY GARRISON IN HISPANIA. I'M NOT NEEDED HERE ANY LONGER. THE GAULS KNOW THEY'RE BEING WATCHED. THEY WON'T MAKE ANY MOVE

YOU CAN TRUST MY MEN! THEY DON'T GO BARKING UP THE WRONG TREE!

...BACK AT ROME, CAESAR'S TRIUMPH IS A HUGE SUCCESS, AND EVEN HIS CAPTIVE AUDIENCE CAN SCARCE FORBEAR TO CHEER.....

Capitol! Capitol!

PAF PAF PAF PAF PAF!

AND CAESAR, DELIGHTED BY THE APPLAUSE OF THE CROWD, MAGNANIMOUSLY SETS THE BARBARIAN CHIEFTAIN FREE

I SUPPOSE IT'S BECAUSE HE'S CLAPPED IN CHAINS

YES, IT WAS A CHAIN REACTION

18B

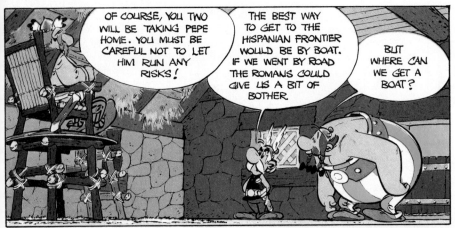

23

LOOK, ASTERIX! HE'S BROUGHT DOGMATIX! WE MUST TURN BACK!

WE CAN'T DO THAT, OBELIX. WE HAVE A FOLLOWING WIND; WE MUST MAKE THE MOST OF IT

SEE WHAT I MEAN? THEY'RE AT IT AGAIN!

HAHAHAHA

HAHAHA HAHA

A FEW MINUTES LATER...

WHAT DO WE EAT ON THIS VOYAGE, UNHYGIENIX?

FISH, OBELIX. WE'LL CATCH IT AS WE NEED IT

WE ALWAYS SEEM TO BE ON ABOUT FISH THESE DAYS!

¡I WANT BOAR!

YOU'LL EAT WHAT'S PUT IN FRONT OF YOU!

HEY! A SAIL!

WE COULD ASK THEM FOR PROVISIONS...

OBELIX, DON'T BE SO PIG-HEADED!

¡IF WE DON'T, I'M GOING TO HOLD MY BREATH, HOMBRE!

!?!

ALL RIGHT, ALL RIGHT! AFTER ALL, WE REALLY SHOULD HAVE BROUGHT SOMETHING TO EAT...COME ON, UNHYGIENIX, LET'S GO!

ONLY A FISHING BOAT... JUST SMALL FRY. BUT THERE MAY BE A CATCH IN IT

CAN'T YOU SEE ANYONE WE COULD ATTACK?

HUH! IT'S NOT WORTH BOTHERING WITH. WE'VE JUST TAKEN ON STORES AND WE'RE FULL OF SALT WILD BOAR!

THAT FISHING-BOAT'S ALTERED COURSE! SHE'S BEARING DOWN ON US!!!

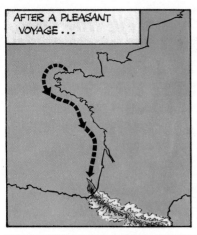

AFTER A PLEASANT VOYAGE...

AT LAST...

THE PATH MUST BE OVER THERE, BEHIND THOSE DUNES. YOU CAN EASILY GET INTO HISPANIA THAT WAY

THANKS! HAVE A NICE JOURNEY HOME, UNHYGIENIX!

GOOD LUCK!

LOOK AT THAT, OBELIX!

23A

HEY, YOU! THIS IS A QUEUE, YOU KNOW! YOU CHAPS IN SPORTS CARTS THINK YOU OWN THE ROAD!

WHAT ARE YOU DOING HERE?

YOU'RE A BIT WET BEHIND THE EARS, AREN'T YOU, BY TOUTATIS? WE'RE ON OUR WAY TO HISPANIA!

WHAT FOR?

FOR OUR HOLIDAY, OF COURSE! THE EXCHANGE RATE IS VERY FAVOURABLE FOR SESTERTII, AND YOU'RE SURE TO FIND THE SUN...I MUST SAY PRICES HAVE RISEN SINCE LAST YEAR. THE NATIVES ARE CATCHING ON...

IT'S SPAINFUL!

TOC! TOC! TOC!

23B

BUT WHY ARE YOU ALL WAITING HERE?

IT'S THOSE ROMAN LEGIONARIES ON DUTY AT THE BORDER... THEY'RE HOLDING US ALL UP!

ROMAN LEGIONARIES?... LOOK, COULD MY FRIENDS AND I GET UP IN YOUR MOVING HOUSE AND...

WHAT?!!! YOU CAN JUST GET IN THE QUEUE LIKE THE REST OF US! WE'VE BEEN CRAWLING ALONG LIKE THIS ALL THE WAY FROM *BURDIGALA!

* BORDEAUX

COME ON! CAN'T YOU SEE WE'RE MOVING?

BELT UP! YOU'RE NOT INVADING US NOW!

COME ON!

THE LEGIONARIES WILL HAVE BEEN WARNED ABOUT US... WE'LL HAVE TO SLIP OVER THE BORDER SURREPTITIOUSLY

BASQUE INN
HOT AND COLD IN ALL ROOMS

WE MIGHT GET SOME INFORMATION THERE...

AND WE'RE SURE TO GET SOME FOOD!

GOOD MORNING... IS THERE ANY WAY WE CAN GET INTO HISPANIA WITHOUT GOING BY ROAD?

AND WITHOUT MEETING ANY LEGIONARIES, EH?

I'LL FIND YOU SOMEONE... MEANWHILE, WHAT WOULD YOU LIKE TO EAT? GOAT? HAM? BEAR? CHICKEN IN THE BASQUET?

FISH!

SOON AFTERWARDS

I'VE GOT JUST THE MAN FOR YOU! HE BELONGS TO THE TRIBE OF THE VACCAEIANS. HE KNOWS HIS WAY AROUND THE MOUNTAINS. HE CAN GUIDE YOU

I NEVER KNEW YOU NEEDED TO BE VACCAEIANATED TO GET INTO HISPANIA

EEK! OUCH! HELP!

CLANG!

BONG!

COMING!

YOU'VE GOT NO MANNERS AT ALL!

¡IT'S NOT BAD MANNERS TO BITE ROMANS!

THERE! SEE WHAT A BAD INFLUENCE HE IS?

WHEN YOU'VE QUITE FINISHED ARGUING, LET'S GET OUT OF HERE!

LET'S GET GOING, O VACCAEIAN! WE DON'T WANT TO RUN INTO ANY MORE ROMANS!

WAIT FOR ME! HEY, WAIT FOR ME!

LATER, ON TOP OF THE MOUNTAIN...

COME ON, THEN! WE'RE WAITING!

IT'S JUST THAT... PUFF! PUFF!... YOU DIDN'T GO THE USUAL WAY. I'M LOST

ANYWAY, YOU'RE IN HISPANIA! ALL YOU HAVE TO DO IS GO STRAIGHT ON DOWN, AND YOU'LL BE IN POMPAELO *

HERE'S YOUR MONEY

* PAMPLONA

NO, YOU DON'T OWE ME ANYTHING! I'VE JUST DECIDED TO RETIRE! AFTER TODAY, I'LL HAVE PLENTY OF STORIES TO TELL MY GRANDCHILDREN IN THE LONG WINTER EVENINGS!

WELL, HERE WE ARE IN YOUR NATIVE LAND, PEPE! ARE YOU HAPPY?

¡AY, ASTERIX! ¡EVEN THE ROMANS TASTE BETTER HERE! ¡OLÉ!

32

WE'LL HAVE SOME DINNER AND THEN GO ON. AND NO ONE IS TO BITE ANY ROMANS WITHOUT MY PERMISSION!

THE REPLEAT TOURIST

GOTHIC SPOKEN

WE SPEAK ENGLISH

THIS WILL DO NICELY

SO HERE YOU ARE BACK AGAIN, SPURIUS BRONTOSAURUS!

DID YOU HAVE A NICE TIME IN GAUL?

SPLENDID! THE HOSTAGE IS SAFE AT TOTORUM. WHEN MISSIONS ARE ENTRUSTED TO ME I ALWAYS ....

29A

¡ VERY WELL THEN, I'M GOING TO HOLD MY BREATH!

!?!

OH, ALL RIGHT, ALL RIGHT! YOU CAN HAVE A LITTLE HERB WINE. BUT DON'T BLAME US IF YOU'RE SICK!

TRAVELLING WITH CHILDREN REALLY IS THE END!

?

THE HOSTAGE! THE HOSTAGE IS HERE!

WHAT'S BITTEN YOU? YOU LOOK A BIT OFF COLOUR

I'M ALL RIGHT... IT'S ALL THIS OILY FOOD. I'VE GONE OFF IT

WHERE CAN WE HIRE A CART, LANDLORD?

TRY NODEPOSITON EL SODASIPHON. THIRD TURNING ON THE RIGHT

29B

AFTER SEVERAL HOURS' DRIVING...

¡THERE ARE SOME NOMADS! I LIKE NOMADS, THEY'RE FUNNY. THEY'RE ALWAYS SINGING AND DANCING

WELL THEN, LET'S STOP AND ASK THEM TO PUT US UP FOR THE NIGHT

¡HEY THERE, FRIENDS! ¡COME AND SIT BY THE FIRE AND WE'LL ALL LAUGH AND BE MERRY!

31 A

¡AYAYAYAYYYYY WOOOOE IS MEEEEE! ¿AYAYAYAYYYYY WHY DID SHEEBEEE LEEEEEEAVE MEEEEEEEEE? ¡AYAYAYAYAYYYYYYYYYY!

CLAPCLAP! CLAP.

¡OLÉ!

¡OLÉ!

¡OLÉ!

¡LET THE MERRYMAKING CONTINUE! ¡NOW FOR SOME DANCING!

CLAPACLAP! CLAPACLAP!

CLAPACLAP!

OLÉ!

¡OLÉ!

CLAPACLAPACLAPA CLAPACLAP

¡OLÉ!

TAP! TAP! TAP!

CLAPCLAP!

¡OLÉ! ¡OLÉ!

CLAPACLAPCLAP!

¡OLÉ!

¡OLÉ, GORGEOUS! ¡COME ON, STICK YOUR CHEST OUT!

CLAPACLAP!

I AM! IT'S JUST SLIPPED A BIT!

CLAC!

31 B

NEXT MORNING, OUR FRIENDS CONTINUE THEIR JOURNEY....

IT'S A GOOD THING WE'VE GOT MORE SENSE THAN THOSE TWO SPECIMENS, DOGMATIX!

WOOF!

RRRRRRONNNNN!

ZZZZZZZZ!

EEEEEEK!

¡OLÉ!

CRASH!

AY, AY, AY! AND NO SPARE WHEEL EITHER!

THERE'S A CART COMING

WE NEED HELP. COULD YOU DRIVE US TO THE NEAREST BREAKDOWN WHEEL-WRIGHT?

THE GAULS!

GRRRRR!

DOGMATIX! AREN'T YOU SATISFIED WITH ROMANS THESE DAYS? YOU MUSTN'T GO BITING PEOPLE TOO!

¡HE MAY BE A ROMAN! I'VE SEEN THAT FACE SOMEWHERE BEFORE

I THINK I HAVE TOO

GRRRR

WHERE DO YOU COME FROM, FRIEND?

I...ER...BY JUPI... OH, NOWHERE! I'M A NOMAD! A HAPPY NOMAD, HOMBRE!

¡OLÉ! ¡OLÉ! ¡WOOOOE IS MEEEEE!

CLACLACLACLAC

ANY GOOD?

¡NOT VERY, BUT HIS KNEES MAKE A NICE ACCOMPANIMENT!

RIGHT, THEN. OUR MISTAKE...NOW, IF YOU'D BE KIND ENOUGH TO TAKE ONE OF US TO THE NEAREST BREAKDOWN...

FINE! I'LL TAKE THE LITTLE BOY!

NO, WE NEVER LET PEPE OUT OF OUR SIGHT! WE'LL ALL GO, IF IT'S ALL THE SAME TO YOU

A PLEASURE! ¡OLÉ!

FOILED!

LET'S INTRODUCE OURSELVES. I'M ASTERIX

I'M OBELIX

WOOF!

¡HUEVOS Y BACON!

I'M...ER... I'M OLOROSO EL FIASCO

SOON AFTERWARDS...

THIS IS WHAT WE WANT

OFF YOU GO, BOTH OF YOU! PEPE AND I WILL WAIT

FODDER STATION

CARTS REPAIRED

NO, WE'LL ALL THREE OF US GO WITH PEPE!

OH, ALL RIGHT! I'LL GO ON MY OWN

LISTEN...THERE ARE SOME PEOPLE OUT THERE WHO NEED A CARTWHEEL. I DON'T WANT YOU TO GIVE THEM A CARTWHEEL. IF THEY COME HERE, JUST TELL THEM YOU HAVEN'T GOT A CARTWHEEL

!

AND HERE'S SOME MONEY FOR THE CARTWHEEL!

?

!?

¡BUT HOMBRE, THIS WON'T WORK! ¡I HAVEN'T GOT ANY CARTWHEELS NOT TO GIVE YOU! ¡I'M RIGHT OUT OF STOCK! I'LL HAVE TO ORDER THEM, AND THAT TAKES TIME...

*COCA

*SEGOVIA

*SALAMANCA

*CORDOBA

WE'LL BE IN HISPALIS TOMORROW. IT'S MY LAST CHANCE. AFTER THAT, PEPE WILL BE BACK WITH HIS FATHER, AND MY MILITARY CAREER WILL BE ENDING UP ON THE SAND OF THE ARENA!

STAND AND DELIVER!

?!?

JUST A MOMENT, NOBLE FOREIGNERS. ¡YOU ARE GOING TO HAND OVER ALL YOUR PROPERTY! ¡WE ARE BANDITS, AND I'M SURE YOU WILL UNDERSTAND THAT WE TOO HAVE TO MAKE A PROFIT FROM THE TOURIST SEASON!

SHALL WE GET THEM?

I WANT TO GET THEM TOO!

I'M THE ONE WHO'S GETTING THEM!

WHY DON'T YOU BOTH GET THEM, AND I'LL LOOK AFTER PEPE!

¡COME ON, HOMBRES! WE'RE NOT ON HOLIDAY, EVEN IF YOU ARE. ¡WE CAN'T WAIT HERE ALL DAY!

OBELIX, YOU STAY WITH PEPE. PEPE! BREATHE! JUST A DROP OF MAGIC POTION, AND I'LL GET THEM!

POF! POF! POF!

36ª

GLUG! GLUG! GLUG! GLUG! GLUG!

?

¡HAND IT OVER!

THERE YOU ARE!

COME ON, MEN!

WHAM!

¡OLÉ!

¡OLÉ!

AFTER A SHORT AND UNEQUAL BATTLE...

¡THE TOURISTS ARE FULL OF BEANS THIS YEAR!

YES, OUR COOKING MUST HAVE IMPROVED NO END

THE MAGIC POTION THAT GIVES SUPERHUMAN STRENGTH! THE FAMOUS MAGIC POTION! IT'S MY LAST CHANCE!

SCB

NIGHT HAS ALREADY FALLEN WHEN OUR FRIENDS ARRIVE IN HISPALIS, THE CAPITAL OF VANDALUSIA. THE MAGNIFICENT CITY IS FULL OF GAIETY. IT IS A HOLIDAY!

YOU'RE IN LUCK; I'VE GOT TWO ROOMS LEFT, NEXT DOOR TO EACH OTHER

I'M GOING TO SLEEP IN DOGMATIX'S ROOM

ME TOO!

ALL RIGHT, THEN, WE'LL SHARE THE OTHER ONE

SPLENDID! SPLENDID BY JUPI... BY OLÉ!

DINNER IN THIS TYPICAL VANDALUSIAN INN IS A CHEERFUL OCCASION

The roads are improving, They're working on them!

A proud and haughty race!

Thin-skinned!

Attractive prices, but they're rising

They've cottoned on!

The cooking's much better these days

TODAY'S MENU IS SAUSAGE, SAUERKRAUT AND BEER

LET'S GO TO BED... WE SAY GOODBYE TOMORROW, MY DEAR AMONTILLADO EL AMOROSO!

OLOROSO EL FIASCO

GOOD NIGHT

GOOD NIGHT

NOW FOR THE MAGIC POTION! THEN I'LL BE THE STRONGEST, AND I CAN GET HOLD OF PEPE AND TAKE HIM BACK TO GAUL

FISH? YOU MUST BE OFF YOUR ROCKER! WHERE DO YOU THINK I'M GOING TO GET FISH AT THIS TIME OF NIGHT?

WHAT ARE YOU DOING WITH THE MAGIC POTION?

DOGMATIX! BREATHE! KEEP YOUR NOSE OUT OF THIS!

STOP THIEF!

SCHLANG!

BRONTOSAURUS! WHAT ARE YOU DOING HERE IN CIVVIES?

THE DOPE! THE DOPE!

INSULTING ME ARE YOU? ME, YOUR OLD COMRADE IN ARMS?

THAT GAUL! DON'T LET HIM GET THE DOPE!

HMM... THIS IS AS CLEAR AS MUD! LET'S GO AND SEE THE COMMANDER-IN-CHIEF

SOON AFTERWARDS, IN THE C-IN-C'S OFFICE...

WELL, BRONTOSAURUS? YOU WERE IN CHARGE OF A HOSTAGE, AND NOW I FIND YOU BACK HERE, IN CIVVIES, KICKING UP A ROW... I SUPPOSE THE HOSTAGE **IS** SAFE IN GAUL, EH?

HE STOLE THE HOSTAGE, HE DID, ALONG WITH HIS ACCOMPLICES! IF YOU HURRY YOU'LL FIND HIM ASLEEP IN THE 'TYPICAL VANDALUSIA' INN WITH A BIG FAT GAUL!

I HOPE YOU'RE RIGHT... GO AND FIND THE HOSTAGE, AND HAVE THESE TWO THROWN INTO PRISON!

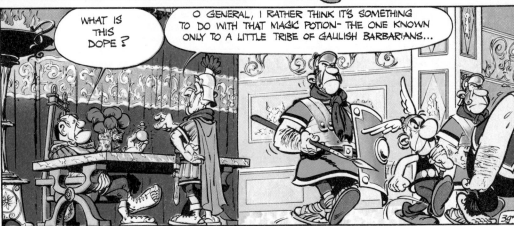

WHAT IS THIS DOPE?

O GENERAL, I RATHER THINK IT'S SOMETHING TO DO WITH THAT MAGIC POTION- THE ONE KNOWN ONLY TO A LITTLE TRIBE OF GAULISH BARBARIANS...

IT IS SAID TO GIVE GREAT STRENGTH!

YOU DON'T SAY!

GLUG! GLUG GLUG! GLUG! GLUG! GLUG!

COME HERE, OBSEQUILIS, MY DEAR FELLOW

THIS IS A REAL HIT FOR OBSEQUILIS!

PAF!

?

?

EXCELLENT, OBSEQUILIS! YOU'VE DONE VERY WELL!

?

SHANKSH, O SHENERAL!

SEND IN ANOTHER AUROCHS, ROMAN. THIS ONE'S FINISHED

NO! I ASK PARDON FOR THIS BRAVE AND CHIVALROUS MAN!

GRANTED! I CAN REFUSE NOTHING TO THE HALF-SISTER OF JULIUS CAESAR'S COUSIN BY MARRIAGE

¡OLÉéé!

PARDON THIS MAN TOO!

VERY WELL, BUT HE'S DISMISSED FROM THE ARMY

I'M GOING TO MAKE MY CAREER IN THE ARENA! SPURIUS BRONTOSAURUS IS NO MORE! THIS IS EL HISPANIES, THE *AUROCHERO!

¡OLÉÉéé!

* NOT AURCHEADOR, AS IT IS OFTEN MISTAKENLY EXPRESSED

THANKS TO THE DIRECTIONS GIVEN BY THE GRATEFUL BRONTOSAURUS, ASTERIX ARRIVES AT PEPE'S VILLAGE, WHICH IS BEING BESIEGED BY THE ROMANS

ASTERIX! HERE I COME!

OBELIX!

WASH OUT! IT LOOKSH ASH IF THEY'RE GOING TO BREAK OUT!

ASTERIX! I'VE BEEN SO WORRIED!

TCHRAAA

COME ON! LET'S GET BACK TO THE VILLAGE! THEY'RE ALL WAITING FOR YOU!

WASH OUT! IT LOOKSH ASH IF THEY'RE GOING TO BREAK IN AGAIN!

SURE ENOUGH...

RIGHT, LESHIONARIESH! WE'LL HAVE A SHANGE OF SHTRATESHY! WE'LL BUILD FORTIFIED CAMPSH ALL ROUND THE VILLASHE, AND KEEP WASH, AND NOT SHTART ANY FIGHTSH, BY SHUPITER!

PRINTED IN BELGIUM BY
proost
INTERNATIONAL BOOK PRODUCTION